DEPTHS OF THE HEART

*11 Fictional Short Stories Written
By Young Incarcerated Juveniles*

Second Chance Publishing

Copyright © 2000
Second Chance Publishing
All Rights Reserved.

No part of this book may be
reproduced in any form, except for
the inclusion of brief quotations in
a review or article, without permission
in writing from the author or publisher.

Library of Congress Control Number: 00-93548
ISBN: 0-9706028-0-4

Printed in the United States by:
Morris Publishing
3212 East Highway 30
Kearney, NE 68847
1-800-650-7888

Excerpts from
Depths of the Heart

Jordan – "Get over here and stop crying like a baby!" yelled his father. With drying tears on his face, Jordan slowly trudged through the snow to where his father was standing. They began to walk down a path. Jordan asked his father, 'Where are we going?" He ignored his son's question and continued to walk. Jordan said, "Daddy, it's cold out here." After a few minutes of walking, Jordan's father pulled off his scarf and aggressively wrapped it around Jordan's neck.

A Soldier's Fury – Distance is slowly disappearing between the two sides as they run full force to meet. Silence comes the moment before each side envelopes the other. A whisper can be heard for miles in each direction, but too soon, it ends. The echoing of crashing metal against metal fills the valley. Ethan winces as a few of the front runners are pulled under the stampede.

The Choice – The small bullet tore through her fragile body killing her almost instantly, a bullet that was meant for me. I couldn't breath, and it felt as if I had been pummeled in the stomach by the fist of God himself, as I dropped to my knees. The screams around me and the sirens in the distance meant nothing. My entire world had been shattered before my eyes. As I held her tiny broken body in my arms, I screamed to the heavens but got no reply.

Acknowledgements

This book was made possible by the generosity of three organizations: **Clackamas County Youth Issues and Planning Committee**, Department of Human Services, Office for Children and Families; the **Walt and Peggy Morey Fund of the Oregon Community Foundation**, Portland, Oregon; and the **Collins Foundation** whose funds were donated through the Salem Art Association. With great appreciation, we thank them for support of our project.

We also wish to extend our sincere thanks to the following: **Nan Minchow** and **Leslie Gertner** (copy editors) for countless hours spent editing; **Dr. Patrick McArthur** (former principal of Lord High School) for his support and encouragement; **Gary Lawhead** (Superintendent of MacLaren Youth Correctional Facility) for authorizing this project; **Linda Nickerson** (Programs Director at MacLaren Youth Correctional Facility) for her fund-raising assistance; **Paul McBride** (Assistant Editor of Second Chance Publishing) for his enthusiasm and assistance; and **Richard T. Camara** (Editor-in-Chief of Second Chance Publishing) for coming up with the project idea, recruiting authors, and managing the details of publication.

Dedication

We dedicate this book to all the young men at MacLaren Youth Correctional Facility. By coming here, each of you has been given an extraordinary opportunity to change your lives from despair to hope. The staff members, campus-wide, who encourage you day in and day out, believe in you and are aware of your potential. In fact, many of us were in similar situations growing up, and we know, personally, about the journey from despair to hope.

It has been our pleasure to copy edit the 11 stories in this book. May you enjoy them as much as we have.

Leslie Gertner and Nan Minchow
Teachers at MacLaren

Dedication

I would like to dedicate the cover artwork to my high school art teacher, Cindy Nielsen. She has never stopped encouraging and believing in me. Because of her, I am so much better at what I do. Thanks, Mrs. Nielsen. I couldn't have done it without all of your help.

Ivan France

Contents

Samaritan by Jason Thomas 9

One Chance in Time by Richard T. Camara 15

Jordan by R. Skylar K. and Alexzander de Avalon .. 25

Bertoniette by Jorge 31

The Choice by Paul McBride 35

A Soldier's Fury by Richard T. Camara 41

Living in Exile by Scott F. 47

Season of Dreams by James Lee 55

Cold as Ice by Paul McBride 59

Cries of Tomorrow by David M. Mosley 65

All Through the Night by Richard T. Camara 79

Dedication

I would like to dedicate this story to Jonnie, Sherry, Jessica, and Jaymye Thomas. I love you.

Jason Thomas

Samaritan
by Jason Thomas

If you dare, you can come with me on a trip down South Street and smell the stench mixed with sweat, filth, and blood. Take a walk through the alleys and meet some of the most savage and foul swine living. Throughout the day you will hear the bloodcurdling screams of the raped and beaten, the gun blasts of the territorial drug lords, the moans and groans of the heroin-famished addict, and the cry for death's mercy. As you look around and see the graffiti blanketing the small, local, commercial shops, be sure to stay out of the path of the beggar in his tattered clothes soliciting for cash. Under the rags is sure to be a rusty, disease-covered dagger waiting to make you another permanent resident of the streets.

In the fifteen years I have lived in the alley between the laundry shop and the strip joint, right off South Street and Pandemonium, I have seen murder, rape, and beatings, as well as had my part in them. I had never seen anything good happen on South Street until last Saturday.

It was about nine in the evening when any well-to-do citizen knows better than to be out on these streets. The only people who come through these parts at that time are those on the prowl or somebody who cannot avoid South Street as a passageway to their destination. I was drinking my evening fifth when I first heard the screams. They were screams of distress, and I immediately knew something was going down. The screams were as common place on

South Street as the jubilant laughter of toddlers playing in the suburban neighborhoods. Years of experience in the tough streets told me to go about my business and ignore the commotion. Too many times somebody stuck their nose into something that was not their concern and wound up dead. But tonight something tugged at me to take a look at what was going on.

When I peered out of the alley and into the street, I saw three masked men mercilessly beating a middle-aged white man who lay shielding his head. They struck him relentlessly with bats until I was sure he was dead. One of them rummaged through his pockets for something, and then took off. The man laid on the streets a bloody pulp, whimpering softly as he started to die. I stood there pondering what to do. I knew that if I helped him, I would be risking my own life, but if I let him be, he'd die for sure.

As I stood there, a young woman came walking down the street. She was dressed in a tight skirt and halter-top. Her flashy makeup was pasted on her face and seemed to proclaim her occupation as the neighborhood prostitute. I had seen her many times before. Her pimp and I had served time together in Lament Correctional Facility, and I had even had the privilege of purchasing her services on a few occasions. When she came within sight of the lifeless body, she quickly crossed the street, not even taking a moment to glance in his direction.

I ducked into the alleyway to avoid being seen. I heard footsteps and peered around the corner to see the local church minister approaching. I felt relieved. Here was somebody I thought might help. So many times he had come to sermonize Jesus to us homeless. But, when he came to the slumped body, instead of helping him, he paused and walked right around him without taking a second look. I wasn't that surprised. It was common to hear people preach about helping others and not do a damn thing themselves. The man now laid motionless on the sidewalk.

    I found myself thinking: *what can I do about this? I really don't have to stick my head in the situation. I should know better. What happened when Loony Len tried to help that hooker being raped? Ended up in some dumpster, all cut up. I don't have to do a damn thing! Let him die! After all, there is no telling why the guy got beat down. Maybe he was trying to buy drugs or get a prostitute. I get tired of those rich folks who just come down here to take advantage of all the sleazy business that goes on. They preach about cleaning up the area only to indulge in its immorality. Maybe it would do the neighborhood good for somebody like that to die. Yeah, I'm not going to do a thing for that stuck up jerk. I'll let 'em die! Serves him right. But then again, what if he was truly innocent? It would be wrong for me to sit and let him suffer like that, but what has he done for me? Those rich folks sit on top of the hill in their fancy cars and homes not doing a damn thing for me.*

    For what seemed like the longest time, I battled about what I should do. Finally, I got off my stoop and walked over to the body. In all my years in the streets, I had never seen such a mangled sight, so bloody and ragged. I checked his pulse to see if he was still alive. I must admit my heart sank when I got a pulse. I looked around to maker sure nobody was looking, then hoisted the mutilated body upon my shoulder and proceeded to walk down South Street.

I was scared, but something told me I was doing the right thing. For the first time in a long time, I felt a sense of pride in what I was doing. On one hand, I knew if one of this man's assailants spotted me, I'd be a dead man. But after years of drug dealing, stealing, and robbing, I knew I was doing something right for once and could have cared less about the man's attackers.

An hour later, as the paramedics loaded the body onto the ambulance, I felt like I had gained a part of my soul I had lost years ago. I returned to my shabby home in the alley between the strip joint and the laundry shop with a sense of pride that night. For the first time, I saw something good happen on South Street, something good within myself.

The human spirit is stronger
than anything that happens to it.

C.C. Scott

Dedication

Faith is something I've always lacked, faith in my talents and faith in myself. As a child, I dreamed of becoming a great man. I imagined myself a well-liked person with many wonderful accomplishments. When I became a teenager, I lost those dreams and followed a path that led to self-destruction.

I was blind to so many things and to the people who tried to help. I can remember so many who reached out a hand to a young man and were only sorry for doing so. Many people had the faith in me I could never find. In a way, this is my thank you to them. If I had just one of those chances you all gave me, I would take it and make you proud. I'm grateful to you all. I know that I burned bridges and made many of those who helped me, dislike me for my deeds.

I've finally found faith in myself, and I dedicate this story to all of you. I apologize for who I was and hope you look toward the future as I am. I've found those childhood dreams once again, and this is only the first of many accomplishments.

Richard T. Camara

One Chance in Time
by Richard T. Camara

Rain fell from the overcast sky. It had been six hours since the funeral had ended. Another two hours had passed since his best friend had left his side. He was frigid and his suit and coat were thoroughly soaked. On his knees, he knelt on the freshly dug graves. Grasping the fresh dirt in his hands, he cried out. They were gone, and it was the reality of the loss he couldn't accept. Tom was alone, and he knew it was forever going to be that way.

Friends and family had drifted away from the funeral. A few had stayed trying to comfort him, but they, too, had finally given up. As always, his best friend was resilient and wanted to stay, but Tom asked him to leave. He just wanted to be alone in the silence, to try and feel their presence. Other people would only get in the way. Yet, even now, all he felt was a cold loneliness. Silence was the very fabric of what his life had become.

In his head he repeated it over and over: they were gone. Just a few weeks before, they were laughing, happy people. Now that they were gone, he saw that he had lived his entire life for them, and he wanted that life back. His best friend had told him to take some time away from the company, but he didn't want to. There was only one thing he wanted, but he couldn't have it. In his grief, Tom reflected on days past.

It was the day before Charity's prom. She held her dress in front of her to show him. With glee she repeated her chanting, "Thank you, Daddy! Thank you, Daddy!" A few moments before, she had unwrapped the box that held her surprise. At first, her mother had said she couldn't have it. It was far too expensive, and there were dresses just as pretty for less money. But, Tom had always made it his business to make his family happy. Going out alone on a Sunday morning, he had bought the dress. Watching Charity open the present and seeing her smile was worth the nine hundred dollar price tag.

It was his habit to indulge Charity, and she never really longed for anything. She had a sports car, a cellular phone, credit cards, and everything that was proper for a spoiled daughter to have. He did, however, think she had far too many shoes, although he couldn't protest too much; his wife had more.

Tom wanted his family to have luxuries. A few years back when they were financially struggling, they never complained about their own sacrifices. Now that he was well off, Tom intended to see the two people he loved most, enjoy life.

He knew he led a gifted life: a successful business with Roger, his best friend since third grade; his beautiful wife, Jessie; and a daughter who would succeed much younger in life than him. He was truly blessed.

His world collapsed the night he stayed late for a meeting with a client. Charity and Jessie went out to dinner and decided they would see a movie. The officer said the driver of the truck wasn't paying attention and jumped a red light. Since the accident, Tom had been to the intersection several times; it was now the bane of his existence.

"It wasn't fair!" He beat his hands on the dirt.

"It is never easy," someone replied. "I've seen it a hundred times, and it's never easy."

The unfamiliar voice came from behind. The presence of a man surprised Tom, and he tried to pull himself together. Bringing his hands up to wipe the tears, he saw the dirt on his hands and wiped them on his tie. Standing, he felt the wetness of his clothes sticking to him and the dirt clinging to his pants.

As he turned, he saw the intruder standing in a gray suit with a black trench coat. Tom recognized him as someone who had been at the funeral. He didn't know how this man knew his wife or daughter, and he didn't care. He just wanted to be alone.

"Can I help you?"

"Actually, Tom, the question is, how can I help you?"

"What do you mean? Who are you? How did you know my wife and daughter?"

"I didn't."

"Then, why are you here?"

"I'm here for you, Tom."

This was ridiculous, and he was feeling irritated. He wanted a straight answer, and he was getting everything but one. The stranger walked toward him. Tom didn't feel alarmed.

"You're soaked straight through, Tom." His words echoed a genuine concern.

The man's hand brushed against the sleeve of Tom's coat. A warm sensation filled him, and the bitter cold that had been his companion for the last few hours was gone. Looking down at his sleeve, it was dry. All of his clothes were dry. The rain was still falling everywhere except on him. Reaching out his hand, Tom opened his palm to catch the rain but felt nothing.

"Rain is such an inconvenience sometimes," the stranger commented.

"Who are you?" Tom asked in awe.

"Only a friend who is offering you a chance. The chance to have your life back, to hold your daughter, to kiss your wife. I can offer that."

Tom knew the words were madness. There was no possible way to have his life back. Closing his eyes, he had to think. Opening them again, he stood in new surroundings. It was the street corner that bordered the intersection where the accident had occurred. The stranger stood next to him. Cars drove through the intersection unaware of the tragedy this place held for Tom.

"How did we get here?"

"I told you. I'm here to give you a second chance."

There was something in his voice that held a comforting truth.

"Are you an angel?"

The man smiled. "Not with halo and wings, but in a way, yes. Do you believe me, Tom?"

Tom's heart said yes. "I think so."

"Good, then we can continue. I can turn back time to save your family, but there is one condition."

"Anything!" he cried.

"I will show you the truth about your life. Things will surprise you, things you never knew existed, and may not wish to know. All you have to do is see the truth and decide if you want your family to live."

There was something in his words that frightened Tom, but he knew whatever he learned, it wouldn't stop him from bringing them back. He was certain of that.

"I agree."

The images around him faded as others took their places. He instantly recognized the boardroom of his advertising firm. The massive table was surrounded by major stockholders, and his best friend sat at one end.

"We're in the past now, Tom. This meeting took place a month ago."

"Then, why am I not there?" asked Tom.

"You were not meant to be there."

"Can they see us?" Tom persisted.

"No, they cannot."

A new curiosity filled Tom. What was this gathering about? His best friend stood and began to address the stockholders.

"We all know why we're here. Even though some of these proceedings will be difficult, they must be discussed for the future of this company. In the past few months, we have seen a slump in sales. There's a simple reason for this: Tom has been making some very poor decisions and has lost his edge. If something isn't done soon, there might not be a company to save."

Pausing, Roger took a breath.

"I hate doing this to my friend, but if our profit margin doesn't start coming up soon, it may never come up again. I ask for a vote. Will you stand with me and place your trust in me? Will you let me take this company into a new era of success?"

The vote was unanimous. In two months time, they would take over the company. The stockholders had shifted their alliance from Tom to Roger.

The meeting ended, and Roger headed to his office. Tom

followed him in silence. It was all so unbelievable. He was seeing a completely different man than the Roger he knew. Thinking it over, Tom had noticed a decline in the company's revenue, but he had been working on a plan with Roger which would have doubled the profit margin.

"What does this have to do with my daughter and wife?" Tom muttered.

"All in good time, my friend. The truth has to be fully seen before you make your decision."

Decision! What was this guy talking about? Nothing was going to change the way he loved Jessie and Charity.

It caught him off guard to see his wife in Roger's office, sitting in a chair with a drink in her hand.

"So, did they buy it?" Jessie asked with a hopeful smile.

"Completely. They have no idea that I have been deliberately sabotaging the business."

No! It couldn't be! His wife was in on it? Why? How? All of Tom's emotions pulled into his stomach, and he felt weak.

Jessie stood and walked over to Roger. Wrap-ping her arms around him, she began to softly kiss him. In between kisses, she spoke. "With the company gone, Tom won't have any money, and I will divorce him. He was always too naive to see what was right in front of him." The two began kissing more deeply.

Tom backed up, closing his eyes. No! No! He repeated it over and over. She had always given him such happiness and support. Had she lied to him all these years? Keeping his eyes closed, he put his hands over his face and cried.

As he pulled his hands from his eyes, Tom realized they were standing in a clothing store. Immediately, he recognized his daughter. She was giggling and talking with her friends.

He wanted to rush out and embrace her. He missed her so much. Silently, he watched his daughter and her friends.

"Charity, do you think your dad will buy that dress?"

"Oh yeah. He hates it when I'm sad. I'll mope around for a few days, and he'll buy it."

"Didn't your mom say no?" another girl retorted.

"Yeah, but dad can't stand to see his baby upset. How do you think I got the Porsche? There are times when my mom says no, but I know I can work my dad. He's a sap. A few tears, and he'll buy me anything I want."

"You're so bad, Charity."

"Well, I guess I am, but my dad's loaded. Why not use his money for something important. Who else could be more important than me?"

His wife and daughter seemed so different. Everything about his life was a lie. Turning to his companion, Tom had tears in his eyes. Shaking his head, he watched as his surroundings changed again. They were suddenly back at the street corner where it all began.

"Where are we now?" Tom asked.

"In a few minutes, your wife's car will pass through the intersection, hitting the truck. Do you want me to save them, Tom?"

Did he? They were already dead and he hated them for lying, for playing him the fool. They weren't the people he thought he knew. He saw the blue BMW come toward the intersection. There was only a short time to decide. He felt so empty inside, although he realized his love for them was surfacing through the pain. It was love, and no matter what they had done or who they were, he loved them still. The car began to enter the intersection.

"Save them."

The BMW drove through, as did the truck. Instead of a collision, the truck passed straight through the car, without incident. For the last time, Tom had shown them his love.

The turning point in the process of growing up is when you discover the core strength within you that survives all hurt.

Max Lerner

Dedications

I dedicate this story to my old man, who has finally found his lost son. I love you.

R. Skylar K.

I dedicate this story to my grandmother who recently passed away. She always encouraged me to go beyond what I thought I was capable of, especially in music and writing. I also want to give thanks to my mom and Heather for reading and supporting my ideas over the years. Other people I am grateful to for their support are Mr. Anderson, Mrs. Nueffer, Mr. Wenz, Mrs. Fenderson, and Mrs. Gertner. And also a special thanks to a special friend, Jamie Hall.

Alexzander de Avalon

Jordan

by R. Skylar K. and
Alexzander de Avalon

He heard his mother arguing, then crying in her room, but continued to play with his wooden blocks on the trailer floor. A cold chill folded over him when his father came out of the room yelling, "We can't handle this responsibility, and you know that!"

His mother replied, "I don't care anymore, just leave!"

Quickly, his father picked him up, but the boy resisted and dived towards his blocks saying, "No, Daddy! No!"

"Come on, we're going for a ride," his father said.

"Where are we going?"

His father snapped back, "Just go get your damn jacket on."

Not knowing what to do, Jordan stood still and looked at his blocks.

"Get your damn jacket on now!" he screamed.

With a shudder, Jordan leaped to the corner toward his bedspace, fumbling for his favorite jacket. His father's second attempt wasn't resisted by Jordan, and he was carried to the door with his New York Giant's jacket and blocks in hand.

Jordan's mother followed them out with a half empty bottle of Wild Turkey. She stopped at the end of the broken down porch, barely mustering enough strength for a normal wave good-bye to her son.

While getting into the family car, an '84 Ford pickup, Jordan and his mother became locked in a helpless gaze.

"Why is Mommy not coming, Daddy?" Jordan asked his half drunken, edgy father. No reply came from his father's lips, but he turned on the radio to drown out the cries of Jordan as they sped off.

Five miles out of Prince Charles, Jordan's father angrily asked, "Why are you still crying?"

Jordan, shaking from his tears, shrugged his shoulders and curled his knees to his chest burying his head.

Enraged by his son's behavior, he turned suddenly off the highway, down a side road. The force of the unorthodox turn jerked Jordan to the side in his oversized seatbelt.

Jordan asked, "Where's Mommy, Daddy?"

His father snapped, "Where is she? Why? Why does it matter?" not wanting an answer.

"I want my mommy," he attempted to say, but his father took another sharp turn down an old logging road. Finally in response, his father said, "Deal with it."

After another five miles of unwanted country classics and bumpy terrain, the pickup stopped on the shoulder ten miles from a nearby town. Jordan looked up out of his ball hoping to see his mom and home. Disappointed, he slumped down never letting go of his blocks. He then felt a movement next to him and looked up to find his father drinking from a shiny metal flask.

Freshly pumped with anger, Jordan's father pushed him, told him to get up, and said, "Put your coat on; it's cold outside."

Jordan mechanically did what he was told and followed his father out the driver's door.

Immediately, Jordan walked to a patch of snow under a giant maple tree.

"Get over here and stop crying like a baby!" yelled his father. With drying tears on his face, Jordan slowly trudged through the snow to where his father was standing. They began to walk down a path. Jordan asked his father, "Where are we going?" He ignored his son's question and continued to walk.

Jordan said, "Daddy, it's cold out here."

After a few minutes of walking, Jordan's father pulled off his scarf and aggressively wrapped it around Jordan's neck.

Jordan started to sing Christmas carols as they continued walking.

His father stopped in an area surrounded by giant maples covered heavily with bright white snow. The ground was rocky and clear under the trees.

Jordan sat on the cold ground and curled into his ball. His father pulled out his flask and took a long pull to take off the chill. He shuddered and said, "Wait here. I'll be right back," and started to walk down the trail.

Jordan nodded his head and said, "I love you, Daddy."

Jordan's father stopped, turned around, and looked deeply at Jordan, frozen in thought. He opened his mouth to say something, but instead, slowly nodded and continued to walk down the path toward his truck.

Jordan then started to play with his blocks, but his hands were too cold, so he tucked them deep into his pockets. He looked around for a sign of his dad but could not see him anywhere.

A sense of shock overcame Jordan. He stood up, and in desperation called out, "Daddy, where are you?"

Nothing. Nothing responded to his calls except for a

gentle breeze that rustled through the trees. He decided to take the path toward the truck.

Jordan saw his father's truck from a distance and started to run toward it. Stumbling down the path, Jordan stopped at the sound of the engine starting.

Jordan cried out, "Wait, Daddy!"

Not hearing the distant sounds of his son, the father drove off, leaving a trail of blue smoke behind. Jordan continued to run after the truck but stopped when it turned out of sight.

Jordan sat down on a nearby rock, curled into a ball, and began to cry.

He remembered his toys, but it was too cold to play. He thought of his mother's presence and the love in her voice. He said in a weak voice, "I want my Mommy."

Everybody thinks of changing humanity
and nobody thinks of changing himself.

Leo Tolstoy

Dedication

Jorge was a young hispanic male who was with us a short while. With his quiet, friendly manner, he was always a pleasure to have in the classroom. After his release, we tried to contact Jorge to write his dedication page. Our request came back with a no forwarding address stamp on it.

Bertoniette
by Jorge

A little boy lies on a dirt floor in the back room of a three-room shack on a dark street. He lives in a poor, hopeless country with his family, including grandparents, aunts, uncles, and cousins. He knows all about illness, sadness, and desperation based on what he sees and hears everyday.

This little boy has hopes of one day having his whole family sit down and eat dinner together. Most nights only half of his family gets fed, and the rest must wait for another day. He dreams of one day having bread with the family meal, so much bread that there will be some left over for the next day.

This little boy has learned to do many things for his family, for his mother and father. He must help with everything, so that his mother and father may have a minute or two of quiet solitude, a minute they cherish and look forward to and silently thank their son for.

This little boy has been in a schoolroom once and hopes to one day go back and learn about the world. There are many wonders he doesn't know exists, not even in his dream world. But for now, he must learn to do the work his parents do, not liking it, but knowing he has to, so his family can survive.

In this hopeless country, many families of men, women, and children, have little more than desperation and illness in their lives, and yet they still dream: they dream of one day having something that will lighten up their dark streets in this poor country; they dream of one day having a place they can call their own – a place they can call home. Families in this hopeless country are living in the gutters and on the streets. Others live under the stars of Mother Nature, sometimes finding shelter and comfort under the trees on country hills and along riverbanks. People will do anything to get a piece of bread to feed themselves for a couple of days. Sometimes they must hide the fact that they have eaten that day, for they may not be fed for days at a time. Fathers and mothers are desperate to earn a couple of dimes to buy some food for the family. Children are not able to get an education because they have to work to help their parents earn a living.

In this poor, hopeless country, there is much desperation but always hope for a better future.

* * *

Most Americans are so fortunate. Feelings of desperation on any given day can be generated by a stalled car on the freeway or having to work late. The contrast of our world and the little boy's is beyond our comprehension.

Opportunity...often it comes disguised
in the form of misfortune, or temporary defeat.

Napoleon Hill

Dedication

I would like to dedicate this story to the overwhelming amount of mind-numbing television that I watched as a child.

Paul McBride

The Choice
by Paul McBride

God, it's so pathetic. I think it would almost be funny if it didn't make me sick to my stomach. All of these people running around down there on the street so concerned with their everyday affairs. Ha! They actually think their lives matter. They think they're in control, yet the people that hire me control everything they do!

I check my watch and once again survey the room around me.

The smell of the stagnant, mildewed air is repulsing. That's good. It means this abandoned apartment building hasn't been used by any living thing in quite some time. If by chance some transient happens to be unlucky enough to stumble through the door, I'll simply kill him and leave the body behind. Those types of people are rarely missed anyway.

I raise the rifle to the window again and gaze through the scope at the entrance to the N.S.A. building. As I line the hairs up with the top button on the valet's jacket, I can read the letters on his nametag as if they were pasted on a forty-foot billboard. I smile as I consider what old Chip down there would do if he knew he had a 7mm sniper rifle aimed at the top left ventricle of his heart. Though I could easily enough end old Chip's measly existence, he is not my target and thus not worth the bullet it would take to kill him.

I lean down and pull out the folder from my attaché case. The name on the front reads Jason Wellington Scott. I've studied this folder and its contents for six month's now, and I'm almost positive that I know our dear Mister Scott better than he knows himself.

Scott kills for money, like me, but there is a difference between him and me. While I will place a bullet precisely on my target or smoothly pull a knife across a throat, severing the trachea and jugular veins simultaneously, Scott will plant a bomb on a stage full of children, just to take out the governor who happens to be making a speech that day. He is the lowest form of scum.

I almost can't contain my rage for this animal, but then I see a man walking down the street with a young girl, I can only assume is his daughter. Suddenly, I flash back to a different place, a different time.

The sun was warm, but the breeze was brisk on my face, refreshing. I made sure she put on a sweater before we left. My little angel, so innocent and carefree. She was so trusting, she thought there was nothing but good in the world. That was m fault. She had always seen how her father was ready to help any stranger in need, ever vigilant to lend a hand. We had always lived together in Dublin, even after her mother left. I loved it there, and it was the only home Moira had ever known.

While she ran ahead on the sidewalk, I was still thinking about the Levingston-Jonscorp merger. It was the first time that an American, government-owned company had attempted to join with a private defense contractor. I was thinking about the peculiar phone call I had received earlier in the week telling me to stay away from the Levingston deal. Then, I heard Moira calling my name. She was jumping up and down ecstatically asking me to lift her up to see through the window of the quaint little doll shop that we walked by most everyday. As I caught up with her, I remembered the eerie voice of the anonymous caller and his ominous warning. But when I saw Moira's smiling face, I forgot all about it and scooped her up in my arms for her to see the beautifully handcrafted dolls in their little French gowns she adored so much. That was my fateful mistake, and it plays in front of my eyes a million times in my endless nightmares.

The small bullet tore through her fragile body killing her almost instantly, a bullet that was meant for me. I couldn't breath, and it felt as if I had been pummeled in the stomach by the fist of God himself, as I dropped to my knees. The screams around me and sirens in the distance meant nothing. My entire world had been shattered before my eyes. As I held her tiny broken body in my arms, I screamed to the heavens but got no reply.

Suddenly, I realize where I am and what I'm doing, as I wipe the tears away. Back then, I was human. Now, I'm nothing more than a monster.

Out of the corner of my eye, I notice Mr. Scott is finally coming through the doors out onto the street. I quickly raise my rifle and line up the sight on his forehead. He stops and smiles while carrying on an idle conversation with Chip. Beads of sweat form on my brow, and my hands begin to shake. I'm so cold, and I don't know why. I try to regain my composure, but it doesn't help. I can't seem to shake the memories of that horrific day. I follow Scott all the way to the cab at the end of the street. I can end his life with a gentle, fluid squeeze of the trigger, but I don't.

I sit there for a second almost hypnotized by what I have just done. I know that Scott deserves to die, but not by my hands. They are covered with enough blood. I drop the rifle to the floor and walk to the door, down the stairs, and out into the street, never looking back.

    I don't know what I'll do. I guess I will start over. I think that's what she would have wanted. For the first time in a long while, I smile when I think of my beautiful daughter, and as I walk down the street, the sun is warm on my face and the breeze is brisk, refreshing.

In the darkest hour the soul is
replenished and given strength to endure.

Heart Warrior Chosa

Dedication

I see fear in every man, selfishness in every man; however, behind those veils there lies a hero. Remember, bravery is faith in yourself.

Richard T. Camara

A Soldier's Fury
by Richard T. Camara

A battle is to be fought this day. Light from the morning sun fills the valley and the surrounding hills. Lines of soldiers stand on either side of the intended battlefield. Armor is heavily worn and swords kept close. Glints of metal flicker on the lines as the sun catches the metal in its light. Men are pressed shoulder to shoulder waiting for the call to battle. Each warring side can see the other, for the distance between them is not great. Generals talk in circles, planning and deciding the fate of these men.

No man physically stands out from another in their purpose, but in some, fear runs high. Each force has equal manpower. The outcome will depend on the training of the soldiers and the will to survive.

Ethan Bane was born in Silverwood Village eighty miles from this valley. In his childhood, playing soldier was the only thing he and his friends truly enjoyed. Those days of acting and dreaming had led him to join the local guard at a young age, a few months hence. A magic had drawn him in, and a blade would be his way out.

Shortly after training, he met a girl. Of course, with her beauty and his weakness for a pretty face, they married. Time had proven her love, and he could only return it with a deepening devotion.

Two days before, Ethan had told Sylvia of his fate. Their last day together was spent in each other's arms, with her sobbing. Time and again he tried to encourage her with false promises, but she knew him well and saw through his words. She pleaded and begged for him to stay, but it was his duty to leave.

Proud was the only word he felt of his station as a soldier. For the first time he was a part of something, someone important, but contemplation of battle had never entered his mind. Peace had been held for so long, the facade tricked him into thinking he would be safe in joining.

War had been declared a month in the past. Rumors had flown as to why. Perhaps it was over land treaties or political insults. Ethan nor any of his kind would never know the truth. It really didn't matter why. Nothing could stop the bloodshed that would come this day.

The call will soon come to charge the enemy. Ethan stands next to his brethren and wishes he was home. Peering around, he wonders how they remain with such allegiance. Are they feeling the same fear that seizes him? An aged, fair-haired man stares at the lines of soldiers across the battlefield. Two men, undoubtedly brothers, laugh at a secret joke, each one coping with their fear. Never before has any of them fought a battle, let alone a war.

Life is so precious to Ethan. Before he had thought of it as a dance with danger, but love has changed his perception. Now, he wishes only to walk off this battlefield alive. If he could run from this, his legs would have long ago begun to work. Only fear keeps him there, and only fear makes him want to desert. A question of emptiness fills him: what would follow if he were to die?

Figures start to gather on the opposite field. Ethan raises his hand to block the sunlight. A trumpet is raised to a man's lips near the lines. Deep in his heart, Ethan bids the man to stop. A trifle sonance arises from the instrument. The power it has is never in doubt, even as it fades.

Screams roar from the far side of the valley. Suddenly, the battle cry echoes around Ethan. The rush of the crowd begins slowly at first. Forcefully, he tries to stand his ground. Fear seeps from every pore as easily as the sweat it mixes with. Unrelenting, the crowd moves faster, and Ethan is swept along. Gradually, the movement turns into a run. Ethan has no choice but to keep pace. Some around him drop their shields and take their swords in both hands. The shields become weapons of disaster bringing down men in the rush. Those tripped by the shields are soon lost under the rushing ocean of men. Looking down at his own shield and sword, he thinks the others foolish for dropping their shields; both items will be useful in the approaching moments.

Distance is slowly disappearing between the two sides as they run full force to meet. Silence comes the moment before each side envelops the other. A whisper can be heard for miles in each direction, but too soon, it ends. The echoing of crashing metal against metal fills the valley. Ethan winces as a few of the front runners are pulled under the stampede. They are crushed to death by the feet of men, enemy's as well as their allies. Swords come swiftly. Death comes swifter.

The fair-haired man who had moments before stood next to Ethan is cut down from a blade to the chest. In return, one of the enemy's men is relieved of his arm by one of Ethan's allies. A scream of joy cries out of nowhere, and Ethan swivels quickly to its origin. One of the men from Ethan's army is slashing wildly, and to Ethan's horror, he is smiling. Laughter bellows from his chest. Bloodlust fills the man.

Paralyzed, Ethan watches people die around him. With flashing eyes and screams, a man rushes, sword high in the air, running toward him. Powerful is the blow, but Ethan's shield holds the attacker at bay. Fear grips the edges of his heart and allows him to fend the blows. Pain shoots through his shoulder, and the shield is lost in the carnage of battle. Time slows as the blood runs down Ethan's arm. A single thought fills his mind: his foe is trying to kill him. Glistening steel strikes at him repeatedly. An anger builds, and a soldier's fury fills his soul.

Deafening is Ethan's cry. The man's blade is blocked by Ethan's own sword. As he spins, he thrusts his blade into the assailant's abdomen. Seconds pass as the astonishment in the man's eyes turns to death. The last moments of the man's life are ignored as Ethan prepares for the next onslaught. No meaning of existence or time is felt as Ethan takes life after life to save his own. Only once during his rampage does he reflect on the lives he is taking, the families that will be crushed by their losses. The fury pushes away every feeling of guilt or remorse. Guilt will not ridicule him.

Moving through the lines of bodies on the ground, a few call for help or just cry in pain, waiting for death's silent release. Ethan recognizes the two brothers, who are now forever fearless, as their bodies lay mangled on the ground. Screams come from men who have been struck down with fatal wounds, but are still alive. A man grabs at Ethan's leg and begs for help. The sash he wears is that of the enemy's. Ethan gives the only help he can: he strikes the man dead.

Time passes in a haze of hatred and death.

Strength seeps from him as the battle ends. Using his bloodstained sword, Ethan holds himself up, fighting the exhaustion. Fury slowly dies down in his soul, back to the place it arose.

Chanting begins all around the battlefield. Screams of victory come from every direction. Ethan raises his weapon high in the air along with his comrades in arms. Victory has been won this day. The chance to live has been earned by this man. The kingdom thinks it is their victory, but Ethan knows it is his. Ethan releases his own victorious cry.

Dedication

The past year has probably been the toughest I have ever experienced, full of self-evaluation and constant change. The support of my family and close friends is what has given me the courage to keep going. There are many people whom I would like to thank for their continued support. Thank you Sarah, Adrienne, and Georgette for showing me how much fun life can be and for helping me learn to be myself. You have given me a very special gift, and I am forever grateful.

I would like to dedicate this story to the three main supporters of my recovery: my mother, my sister, and my best friend, Angie. Thank you for showing me that meaningful relationships do exist and that pain does end. Without you, I would still be lost.

"You may trod me in the very dirt, but still, like dust, I'll rise." – Maya Angelou

"Some of the most wonderful people are the ones who don't fit into boxes." – Tori Amos

Scott F.

Living in Exile
by Scott F.

Cameron West awoke clawing at his throat, coughing, gagging and struggling to draw in a small amount of oxygen he knew would never come. The smoke filled the room, making it impossible to breathe. His lungs burned with the fumes as a reward for each effort. Cameron knew his time was up. With his eyes closed tightly, he prayed to no one that the end would come soon.

But as quickly as it started, it was gone. The smoke, the fire, everything had vanished. Cameron greedily gulped the air, unable to get enough. The episode brought on by the nightmare was over. He collapsed back onto the bed.

When he was able to, Cameron opened his eyes and surveyed the room. The blackness told him it was still very early. After fumbling around on the dresser, he produced his watch. It was just after one. While most people slept, he had given up that luxury a year ago when his life had derailed. Now he was lucky if his senses would numb long enough for him to rest, bringing him momentary relief from his torment.

Today was the one-year anniversary of the accident. When Flight 291 had fallen from the sky, so had his hopes of any kind of normalcy. For the last year Cameron had drowned his pain in a haze of intoxication. But today he would face it head on. Resigning himself to his task, Cameron sat up. The instant pain in his head quickly brought back memories of the previous night.

Cameron had spent the best of the night in a dark hole known as *Sid's*, a bar he had been frequenting. It was a place for one to be alone and forget their troubles. Last night Cameron had consumed probably double his limit before being booted out for fighting. He had stumbled into his run-down apartment around midnight.

Cameron had sold his lakefront home a few months after the accident, unable to live with the haunting memories. He now resided in a shaggy, one-bedroom apartment set above a corner bookstore. It suited his need, which was a place to stay. The nights he made it home from *Sid's*, ended with him passing out on the single mattress that occupied the bedroom. This brought an absence of thought and dulled his pain, except when the nightmares came, which were becoming more often.

The same one had plagued him for the last year. He was flying back from a medical conference in New York. The night was especially stormy with flashes of lightning illuminating the sky every few seconds. Cameron was quietly dozing with his headphones – classical music always soothed him – when he smelled the first hint of smoke. At first he thought some inconsiderate passenger had started smoking, but it soon became apparent that something was seriously wrong. As Cameron looked around, he saw that the few passengers awake were quite aware of the fumes as well. He reached out to a flight attendant as he hurried past, but the man just pushed by on his way to the cockpit. Dark, grayish clouds of smoke were beginning to find their way into the compartment. The pilot came over the intercom trying to sound composed, but the edges of fear could be easily detected. He was saying something about remaining calm, but Cameron barely heard it. Screams of the other passengers were taking precedence as the plane plummeted dramatically. He coughed and gagged as the fumes filled his throat. The plane continued to fall, and Cameron braced himself against the seat, waiting for impact. He screamed.

The scream snapped him back to reality and immediately dissolved the vision. A shudder shook his entire body. He crawled out of bed wanting to rid himself of the sweat that clung to his body. Several empty beer cans scattered on the floor, made the journey from the bed to the shower difficult. Cameron kicked them out of his way as he blindly walked to the bathroom. Standing beneath the steaming water, the last remnants of the nightmare were washed along with his sweat and tension. He toweled off and stepped out of the bathroom.

Maneuvering through the room was quite a bit easier with the bathroom light streaming in. His bedroom was sparsely furnished with a mattress and a small bedside dresser. The room contained no closet. Cameron's clothes occupied a small cardboard box that sat in the corner. The rest of the floor was littered with dozens of empty beer cans. Stepping around the latter, he searched through his belongings for a decent pair of slacks. Most of his wardrobe had been sold along with the house.

After finding a clean pair of khakis and a button up shirt, Cameron finished getting dressed. As he moved out of the bedroom, he took one last look around. There were no pictures or posters of any kind decorating the walls. The only ornate object in the house was Cameron's framed Ph.D. certificate hanging above his bed, the only reminder of the life he once had. Grabbing a small wooden box from inside the dresser, he pocketed it and left the bedroom.

In the kitchen, Cameron removed a small red cooler from a cupboard and filled it with his last six pack. He stood in the middle of the barren kitchen trying to find something else to do before he had to leave. Coming up with nothing, he grabbed the cooler and started out. Cameron paused outside the door and looked back into the apartment. For a second, he was struck by its emptiness. Then, he realized it was appropriate. It reflected the emptiness of his soul. His family was gone and he had nothing. Cameron knew what had to be done. He closed the door and turned his back on his apartment for the last time. He would not miss it.

* * *

Olive Branch Cemetery was set on a high cliff overlooking the ocean. From the parking lot there were two paths. One led to the cemetery and the other to the beach. Getting out of his car, he grabbed the cooler from the passenger seat and set out. The beach path led to an old wooden set of stairs that descended the wall of the cliff. After looking briefly to the rocks below, Cameron headed down the stairs. Once on the beach he found a spot where the warm sand was just barely reached by the lapping waters. He settled in the sand and opened the cooler beside him. Popping the top off his first beer, Cameron took a long hard sip. He drank as the steady morning light began to appear, and he watched the waves lap in and out. It was cold and mechanical. The waves, the world, everything operated without purpose. The world was cruel and unloving. Things were freely given and then ripped away. There was no meaning or reason behind anything.

Cameron did not believe in God. He couldn't. He couldn't stand the logic that everything happened for a reason. He had always seen that as a way to cop out on the pain.

Cameron embraced the pain. He deserved it. Without it, he would have nothing.

Life had taken everything else. His pain was the one thing Cameron could hold onto.

After an hour, Cameron had finished his beers, and he was feeling more ready to face what lay ahead. He got up and staggered back to the wooden staircase, leaving the cooler on the beach. It was time for him to visit his daughters' graves. In the year since the accident, he hadn't been able to bring himself to do it. Today he would.

It was difficult for him to ascend the stairs, but he eventually made it to the top. On extremely unsteady legs, Cameron made it across the small parking lot to the iron gates of the cemetery. The warmth of the dawn seemed to stop at the gates and immediately a chill set in. Once inside, the depression of the place sobered him, and he wished he had more beer. Everywhere he looked there were bright flowers on top of graves. Cameron suddenly realized that he didn't know where his daughters were buried. He had never been here before, not even after the funeral service at Trinity Covenant Church. To this day, Eden, his ex wife, hadn't forgiven him for that.

It was a fairly small cemetery, so it didn't take long for him to find the plaque on the ground that simply read:

Angela & Tymberly West
September 15, 1989 – July 13, 1999
Daddy's little angels

Cameron fell to his knees, and a wretched sob escaped his throat. He laid his forehead on the headstone and wept, his tears falling on the black marble. After several minutes he was able to raise his head. From his pocket he removed the small wooden box and opened it. From inside he withdrew a photograph of his two beautiful little girls on their ninth birthday. They looked lovely and full of life. Their huge green eyes sparkled as they hugged behind their cake. Cameron remembered the day as if it were yesterday. It was the first birthday they had spent without Eden, their mother. He had become a single parent after she'd moved on to "bigger and better things." At that point his daughters had become his life.

From the box he also withdrew two small golden necklaces. On each were the words *Best Friends*. Cameron had bought these to give to the girls on their return from their mother's. Their plane had never made it.

The photograph and necklaces were the only things Cameron had saved to remember his lovely daughters. This was the first time he had pulled them out since the accident. Now, holding them in his hands, all the pain came flooding back as if someone was ripping out his heart all over again. Cameron lay sobbing in the cemetery.

After what seemed like hours, the pain subsided and the tears stopped. Cameron had come here today to give his daughters the gift they never received. On the girls' graves, he placed the two golden necklaces along with their picture. He bent over and kissed the smooth black marble.

"I love you, Angela. I love you, Tymberly," he spoke softly to his little angels. "Daddy's coming home." With that, he stood and walked back to his car.

Cameron started the engine but just sat for awhile. He stared straight ahead seeing nothing, not the ocean or the beautiful morning sky, not the flocks of seagulls, not the guardrail ahead of his car that blocked off the two hundred-foot drop to the beach. Nothing. After a few minutes, Cameron released the emergency brake, put the car in gear. Only one thought ran through Cameron's mind: *Daddy's coming home.*

Dedication

I would like to thank many people for their support during some of the toughest times in my life. **First of all, my sister Jeannie**: where would I be without you? You always picked me up when I was down. **To all my friends and family who never left my side**: thanks for keeping it real. **Kato**: I've been blessed to have you as my bro' since day one.

A lot of people would have never thought that I'd make it with the class of '99. But Mr. Lipner and Ms. Levin saw the light that shined within me. I probably would have never found that if it wasn't for them. Receiving a high school diploma didn't just mean I made it through high school. It meant I made it through a huge obstacle. And finally, I have to thank God for letting my loved ones and me to see this day. Through all the ups and downs, my faith is given to you.

J. Lee

Season of Dreams
by James Lee

Growing up meant constantly having to adapt to new circumstances and new things; however, one thing stayed constant. Just as the fall would always follow summer, I always had a season of football to love and look forward to during high school. Gresham football was a part of me, and the greatest season of my life was also the last time I ever played the game with the team I loved. This was truly my season of dreams.

* * *

Wow! Time had gone by so fast. My final year of high school football was here. It was hard to believe that just three years ago, I had been a freshman scared to death of the huge seniors. I believed they could have competed with the Green Bay Packers. Back then, I cheered the Gresham Gophers onto victory with all my heart, knowing someday I'd be playing under those Friday night lights. That someday was now here, and it was my turn to shine.

The well-known daily doubles had started. For three years I had gone through them, and each year they made me stronger, physically and mentally. The team grew close as the coaches prepared us to play with every inch of our hearts. Gresham always played with their hearts. That's what gave us so much pride and honor in wearing the royal blue jerseys. We may not have been the biggest, strongest, or fastest team in the state, but I guarantee after every practice and every game, each of us walked off that field knowing we gave at least 100%. Every year the Gresham Gophers were feared, and one win over us was considered a successful season for anyone who beat us.

On the night of the opening game, we came running out of the locker room onto the soft, green grass of Stapleton Field. The crowd was screaming, and shivers ran up and down my body. I remember the moment they introduced my name in the starting lineup. The crowd yelled, and I felt so proud as every voice cheered us on. It was my senior year, and if I had been saving the best for last, this had to be it. It was up to me to carry on the tradition of Gresham football.

We beat Park Rose that night 56-0, and remained undefeated the rest of the season. It was a satisfying achievement, but our real dream was to win the state championship. We had a great shot at it, but a power team stood in the way: the Roseburg Indians. Ironically, they were the ones who defeated the Gresham Gophers three years before in the championship game. I remember that sad night the Gophers walked off the field in tears. Now, Roseburg needed to know that Gresham was back to win.

Game night against Roseburg remains crystal clear in my mind. The crowd was as big as ever, and the butterflies were floating around in my stomach. At the opening kick-off, sparks flew as helmets crashed. This was going to be a battle of the two best football programs in the state, and one team would walk off victoriously.

At the half, they led 3-0. I was stunned but had a feeling things would turn around. I was wrong. Roseburg scored two more touchdowns in the fourth quarter. The clock was at 10 seconds, and I remember looking into the eyes of my teammates. Was this for real? Players were approaching me saying we had had a great year, but I was so confused. Tears were rushing from my eyes when the clock hit zero. Roseburg screamed with joy as their crowd ran onto our field. The score was 16-0. That was the first and final loss that ended our season and my career. But despite the pain of losing that night, time has healed the loss.

Gresham football taught me dedication and discipline. It made me a better person, and when I look back, I take pride in every bit of sweat I dropped on that field. And even though that was the last time I wore football pads for Gresham, the incredible memories of those Friday night lights will be with me forever.

Dedication

I would like to dedicate this story to one of my favorite writers, a poet not only on paper, but in life as well. This is one of my favorite poems by him. It gives us identity and purpose, and for that, I thank him.

Fallen Angels

Fallen angels. I've never heard a more beautiful phrase. A term for those of us who love to love. Sometimes we cry, sometimes we fall, but we always wipe our tears and get back on our feet. Those of us who have fallen through the cracks. The people who seem to live through everything, not live, survive. We are survivors, lovers, poets, painters, greasers, scrubs, homeless, and angels. We are fallen, or not. Doomed, it seems, to care for everyone, even the ones we hate. Fallen angels, beautiful.

J.D.H.

Paul McBride

Cold as Ice
by Paul McBride

I was cold as ice, man. I mean, I was tough. At least I thought so, and everyone who crossed me thought the same. Every chance I got, I was hurting someone or myself. Life for me was pumping every poison imaginable into my body, and when someone looked at me wrong, I had to teach 'em a lesson.

Some people tried to blame who I was on my parents, but it wasn't their fault. My dad died before I was born, and my mom was too jacked up on dope to ever really take care of me. I spent most of my life bouncing from one family member to another, getting screwed royally the whole way. After that, it was from state home to state home, but in the system, you don't get screwed as much as you do with your own family. When you're with family, you let your guard down. I mean these are people you can trust, right? Wrong! They just say they love you to your face, then stab you in the back. In the system, you know better than to let your guard down. You know from the beginning that no one gives a rat's ass about you. No one, until Kat.

I still remember when I first met her. Me and some of the guys from the Boy's Home had gone to the community center to hang out and play some basketball. When we walked through the door, I noticed this girl working behind the counter, reading a book. She was a looker, I'm telling you, but that didn't mean much. I'd seen a lot of good looking girls around here, so it wasn't anything new. As soon as we walked in, the guys laid into her, whistling and hollering and trying their smoothest lines. She, nonchalantly, reached under the counter and pulled out a basketball. Smiling, she threw it and told us to go play some hoops without ever raising her eyes from her book. With the moans and groans of exaggerated rejection, the guys grasped their broken hearts and stumbled through the gym doors. Holding the door, I turned and glanced back. She looked at me and gave me the sweetest smile I had ever seen. It caught me off guard, and I darted through the doors.

Standing inside the gym, I was shaking my head trying to figure out what had just happened. Why had I acted like such a moron? She was just a girl, right? Wrong, again. Then, one of the guys yelled that I was holding up the game, so I ran to the court.

We couldn't have been playing for more than a half hour before I went up for a shot and came down on someone's foot, rolling my ankle so badly, I thought I had broken it. A couple of the guys carried me out to the main foyer and set me in a chair. One of them looked up and said, "Hey Kat. Jake, here, busted his leg up pretty good," and then, they were off, back to playing their game.

Kat reached under the counter and this time brought out a first aid kit. She walked over to me and pulled up a chair. Watching her, I noticed how truly beautiful she was. She was wearing a blue polo shirt with the community center's logo and a small pair of khaki shorts that showed her tanned, athletic legs quite well. She wore no make-up, and her shoulder length, blonde hair was tied back in a simple ponytail, with a small portion of her bangs dangling in her face.

She bent over and grasped the back of my heel, gently raising it up to her lap. I winced as the pain shot through my leg. She just laughed and said, "Boy, for tough guys, you sure are a bunch of babies." Before I had a chance to respond, she had my ankle wrapped tightly, and all that was left of the pain was a dull throb. I thanked her under my breath, somewhat ashamed of the way I whined. She looked at me in mock astonishment saying, "Was that a thank you? I don't hear many of those around these jerks, but maybe you're different."

In my smoothest *I don't care voice* I said, "Maybe, maybe not."

She replied, "Oh, *another* tough guy. Well, you know what? I don't think you're that tough. As a matter of fact, I'd bet there's a nice guy in there somewhere. He's just too intimidated to come out. You're not intimidated by me, are you?" she asked smiling.

I blurted, "No!" lying through my teeth, with quite possibly the most fake laugh of all time.

She shook her head from side to side amused by my attempt to save what was left of my bruised and battered pride. As she walked away, and I was admiring the view, she hollered back, "Well, if I don't intimidate you, you should have no problem keeping me company until the end of my shift. That is, unless you have something better to do."

Then, she sat down behind the counter and began reading her book again. At that point I rose from the chair, and on one foot, hopped over to the counter. Teetering on one leg, I was doing my best to seem cool but failing miserably.

After a few seconds, I realized that she was through talking, so I said the first thing that came to mind. "What are you reading?" while actually I wasn't the least bit interested in that.

Looking up somewhat surprised that I bothered to ask, she replied, "It's a book of collected poetry. Would you like me to read some to you?"

I was so mesmerized, I said yes, without even realizing it.

The next few minutes were like a dream as the words rolled off her lips into my subconscience like sweet honey from a comb. All I remember is the tale of a precious love found and then lost. For the first time, I had a feeling in my stomach that I couldn't explain. I just simply wanted to be around her, to hear her every word.

The next few months were a blur, filled with trial and error. Every time I tried my tough guy act, she would shoot me down. I wasn't insulted by her directness, only amazed by her strength. I found myself telling her my life story. I even cried in front of her. I trusted her that much.

To this day I have never doubted why I fell in love with her, but there is not a day that goes by that I don't wonder why she fell in love with me. I asked her once, and all she said was, "I guess you're just lucky," then smiled and fell into my arms. It's amazing how the world works sometimes. This is the happiest that I've ever been, and I'm not high, drunk, or doing dirt.

* * *

Occasionally, I look back at who I was and the things I did, and I feel shame. But that was a long, long time ago, and I still have the woman that I love by my side: the beautiful, strong, intelligent woman that taught me how to love as well as be loved. The woman that helped me through endless trials and tribulations to become the man I am today. The woman who was tough enough to melt a heart as cold as ice.

Dedication

There is a path each of us has been given, although it may not be the path we want. In my time of need, I was confused and made choices that pushed away the only person who really cared about me, because I was afraid of the truth: that death is final and no one can bring a loved one back. Our lives can never be the way they were before. Tragedy happens, and each of us must go on.

There is one person, my sister, who has treated me with such compassion and unquestionable love. My life would have had no direction without her. She has saved me from myself several times over and for this, there is not enough thanks in the world to give her. I cannot express to her all the gratitude I have.

I dedicate this story and all my work to my sister,
Theresa Y. Davis
And to the memory of our mother,
Victoria Elizabeth Mosley.
May we sit on the doorstep of our dreams
And be caught by the love of the sky's harmony
and gentle grace.

All of my love,
David M. Mosley

Cries of Tomorrow
by David M. Mosley

The foyer was narrow and plain. Past the second set of sliding doors, it emptied into a reception area that served as a waiting room. Thankfully, the administration was particular about the air-conditioning. Veronica Thomas felt the temperature drop to a comfortable sweat. She pushed past mothers with screaming babies, angry men yelling obscenities into phones, and irate social workers unable to explain the dynamics of an HMO.

She stopped at the service desk where a pale-skinned woman of about fifty sat with her face half-covered by glasses which must have been rejected almost that long ago. She glanced over the lady's shoulder. Looking down the dark hallway, she saw the red letters stenciled over the only door identifying the chaos within: Emergency Surgery. The severity of the last forty-five minutes finally hit her.

It was every parent's nightmare come true: a call at work from the hospital.

"Your son was brought into Emergency. Please come, right away." The heart races, blood pressure rises, hands start shaking. A simple thought resonated through her: She would sacrifice herself if it meant her son could live an hour longer.

"My son was brought in from school," was all she could manage to say before she felt the wet sting of tears form at the tops of her eyes.

"What's his name, ma'am?" the nurse asked with deep compassion.

"Timothy Thomas," she murmured.

"Right this way," the nurse said, walking toward the restricted access doors.

She led Veronica Thomas to a private waiting room where her most latent fears were described to her by a doctor she had never met. Her only son had been brought in with a gunshot wound to the head.

All the questions, all the possibilities of how and why, collapsed upon her. When she found the strength to ask how it happened, the answer she received was even more frightening than the question.

"Ma'am, I understand you must have dozens of questions, but I really think you should let the police explain. Excuse me," the doctor said as he turned and quickly exited.

Standing at the door was a stocky man in a light T-shirt and shorts, with gray streaks in his goatee and a clean-shaven head, looking more like a bouncer than an officer of the law. He approached with what was either a cocky strut or an aggravated case of hemorrhoids.

Mrs. Thomas sat on an overstuffed loveseat fishing for a cigarette. Her hands shook as she held the cursed nicotine stick to her mouth, searching for a lighter.

"There's no smoking in the hospital," he said. She didn't look up from her purse; a smoking ticket was the least of her worries.

He sat beside her, far too close for her comfort. His badge was hanging from a chain around his neck, declaring him a detective.

"What happened?" she whispered, exhaling a cloud of blue smoke as tears filled her eyelids. "Timothy was at school," she said, as though the words were protection enough.

"Do you own any guns, Mrs. Thomas?" he asked.

She eyed him carefully.

"No, none. Why?"

"Does your husband or anyone else?"

"I have no husband. Now, will you tell me what in God's name is going on?" she demanded.

The detective looked away as she puffed quietly on the cigarette, wishing it would deliver her.

"My name is Mark Ceros, and I'm a detective with the County Police Department. At one-fifteen this afternoon, your son entered his high school cafeteria and allegedly opened fire on some two hundred classmates." Mrs. Thomas's face flushed, darkening her light, almond complexion.

"Ma'am, two teenagers died today and five others were seriously hurt." She fell back, closing her eyes on a moment that would last her as long as she lived.

"How? Why? A gun? Two dead? No! Not *my* son! He's not a killer! He's just a little boy!"

According to Mrs. Thomas, her son was an average teenager, nothing above or below normal. He had stayed on the right side of the law, participating in school events, even playing soccer for his freshman year. He wasn't a jock or an intellectual. He wasn't part of the "in crowd," but he had several friends, all B and C students. He didn't do drugs or alcohol, which said a lot for an inner-city kid.

"Where did the guns come from, Mrs. Thomas?" Ceros asked, flipping a page of his notebook.

"Guns? I've never allowed one in my house!"

"Do you know any friends who own guns or could have bought one for Tim?"

"Not any of my friends, Detective. What's going to happen?"

Ceros could not help but glance away from her bloodshot, amber eyes. She wanted him to tell her it would be all right, but that was not an answer he could give.

"Ma'am, it's not my place to answer that," he sighed. "Let me finish these questions, and I'll be on my way. I realize how hard–"

"No you don't," she said flatly.

"I'm sorry. Is there anyone I can call?"

"A friend already knows I'm here. She'll be over after work."

"Very well, then. Your son allegedly used two guns, a 25-caliber semi-automatic Browning and a 22-caliber semi-automatic Ruger. Do you have any idea where he got them?"

She shook her head unable to find words to describe her shock and confusion. A single word repeated itself in her head: *why?*

Ceros continued. "The serial numbers are being run at the station. We should know by tonight if the guns were reported stolen. Does Tim have a history of mental health problems like depression, sudden loss of interest in activities or sports?"

Mrs. Thomas thought for a moment. Their homelife was typical of a single parent household. His father had abandoned him at an early age, but Tim didn't seem to suffer from the loss. As far as she could tell, he had male role models and heroes. There was no abuse or violence, aside from the father's bad drinking habits.

"Tim was very serious about soccer last year, but all of a sudden, he just stopped playing. I was surprised he didn't try out for this year's team."

"What was he interested in this year? Anything different?"

"No, he spent a lot more time at the Miller's—"

"Who are they?"

"They've been our next-door neighbors for eight years. They have a sixteen year old son named Brad. He's been friends with Tim for years."

Detective Ceros continued questioning Mrs. Thomas for almost an hour on details ranging from daily activities to the last special outing they had taken together. Finally, after much prodding, Ceros realized he would get little more from her that night and concluded with a well-rehearsed and often ignored warning.

"Please, Ma'am, do not speak with anyone about the crime, especially the press. I am available at the number on this card, day or night. Please don't hesitate to call if you think of anything concerning the case or have any questions." He stepped out of the waiting room to Mrs. Thomas's relief.

Left alone, she sat in the private waiting room. The questions how and why could not escape her. She was a parent trapped in the most personal hell imaginable. *Was it something I did? Did I cause my son to become a monster? What if the surgery fails? What if he dies? How will I live without my son?*

She found herself staring at a small, square, end table beside a loveseat. The detective's card caught her eye. She picked it up and placed it inside her pocket. She glanced up at the clock, which was seven minutes slow. It said nine twenty-three. She searched for a blanket to lay over the small couch. Resting her back upon the faded ivory-tinged cushions, she closed her eyes while silently praying for deliverance from the nightmare. The loveseat was only slightly softer than the unpolished, tiled floor.

> *"I'll find you. I'll find you," she whispered. She could feel the breath of another, hot as fire on her neck. She was being chased "I won't let him get you! I won't!" She ran harder and harder. "I must find you! I must!"*
>
> *A figure stood in the far distance, but she felt the hot fire of the other on her, on the walls, on the ground, everywhere. Flames leapt to her face, but she still ran. The ground began to tremble. All she could see was the unrelenting fire, yet she still ran. The flames tried to engulf her. She screamed, "No!" but it was too late. The figure in the distance began to fade into the forlorn darkness. She cried, "Please, please let him live!"*
>
> *"Mama," a voice called out. "I'm sorry."*

"Timothy!" she cried, suddenly sitting up.

"Veronica?" a familiar voice called out. "Are you all right?"

Veronica turned to see the woman enter the waiting room. She held a plate of steaming chicken and mashed potatoes. Until she saw the food, she had not realized her last meal had been an English muffin the previous morning.

"Marie? Is that you?" The lights were dim and she was unable to focus her eyes, yet there was no mistaking the dark-skinned woman now standing beside the loveseat.

"Thank God," she sighed.

"I didn't mean to wake you, but I was sure you hadn't eaten. Here, sit up." Marie handed her a freshly made plate of potatoes and southern fried chicken.

Veronica stabbed at her plate with a plastic fork. "Thank you."

There was a moment of uneasy silence as each woman tried not to think about the events that had led them there.

"I rushed over as soon as the diner closed. Will has the kids at his place." Marie cracked a slight smirk at the mention of her ex-husband babysitting their two children.

"I'm sorry," Veronica said.

"For what? I'm not. It's about time he took care of his kids during a school week. He needs to experience what I do every Monday through Friday." Marie looked at the pile of food wrappings. She regretted putting such an emphasis on school week.

"Would you like some lemonade? I brought some from the diner," Marie offered, trying to change the subject.

"No. What time is it?"

Marie turned to the clock.

"Almost two forty-five."

"The doctor said surgery would be over between three-thirty and four. You feel like walking?"

Marie smiled. "Veronica, you think I've been running a downtown diner for the past nine years and don't like to walk? I live to walk. Come on."

If there was one thing in this unforgiving world that could be counted on, it was Marie's ability to turn her eye from anything painful and bring joy instead.

The lights were dim and the hallway was vacant. Veronica badly wanted another cigarette, but thought better of lighting up in the hospital in front of Marie. They reached a skybridge connecting the main building to the food court. Veronica paused to look out the west windows. Marie broke her casual stride and stood next to her friend.

"I don't know what I'm going to do, Marie," she said softly, gazing toward the distant stars.

Marie looked at Veronica's face lit by the full summer moon and tapped at the thick glass enclosing them.

"We never know, Ronnie. Some believe it's destiny. Some believe it's God who lays the path to our future. But for each of us, one thing reigns true. We never know how we will survive from one crises to another. After Will and I divorced, do you think I knew how I was going to raise two children and run a diner without a husband? Please. I went to bed six nights out of seven leaving Will's lunch in the refrigerator." She paused for a moment. Veronica was still staring into the darkness.

"I finally got a grip on myself when I realized I had a refrigerator full of stir-fried lunches."

They both giggled.

"I like to think of life as a kind of road. No one knows where the road will lead, and every so often you will hit interchanges, bridges, and potholes... lots of potholes, but the purpose is to get to the end of the road."

"Why? What's there?" Veronica questioned.

"I can't tell you. It's different for everyone. But it will be better than anything you've ever imagined." They stood still for several moments. Veronica gradually turned from the windows and continued across the skybridge.

Since the cafeteria closed at midnight, the late night visitors typically amassed in the food court around the vending machines. Veronica was lost in thought until they reached the court's entrance. The room was not too large but enough space was provided between the tables for private conversations. One wall was lined with six vending machines full of junk food. There were an additional three for beverages. Two TV's were arranged at opposite ends of the room for viewing network channels only. Veronica reached into her purse and pulled out a five dollar bill. She placed the bill in the roller and pressed the code for a peanut butter cup, twice. The bright orange wrappers fell into the dispenser, and she picked up her change.

The room's decor was depressing: faded beige walls broke at unequal widths, the windows were dirty and cheap, and the short-backed chairs were covered with the most ghastly shade of purple. They sat at a gray formica table. The television was on in the background tuned to the news, which neither of them noticed.

"I just want to thank you, Marie. I know it's a lot for you to be here."

"I already told you that Will offered to take the kids, and I could leave the diner closed until this heat wave lets up. I haven't had a customer other than the old wino who comes in for the air-conditioning, and I'm tired of trying to explain to him why I don't sell alcohol."

They each nibbled at their peanut butter cups in silence. In the background, they could hear the news anchor mention the words "high school shooting," and instantly, they regretted leaving the waiting room. Despite their reluctance, they stared in silence and listened to the report: "...In what is becoming all too common in American high schools, another school shooting took place early this afternoon.

Sixteen year old Timothy Eugene Thomas allegedly opened fire on his fellow classmates at Central Point High School, around one o'clock this afternoon. Killing two students and wounding five others, the young Mr. Thomas allegedly walked into the crowded cafeteria, sat a black gym bag on a table, and screamed, "You did this to yourselves!" He then pulled out two semi-automatic weapons: a Browning 25 caliber pistol and a Ruger 22 caliber long rifle."

The television screen then shifted to family photos of a handsome, muscular, young man and a fair-skinned, young woman with light, wavy hair and cheerful eyes.

"Seventeen year old Michael Harding and fifteen year old Kimberly Johnson were reported dead on arrival at Central Point Medical Hospital. The assailant fired a reported thirty-two rounds before turning one of the guns on himself. Michelle Harding, Michael Harding's younger sister, was also reported wounded in the gunfire and is currently under observation. Mr. Thomas is currently undergoing surgery at Central Point Medical. The four other victims are all reported in good condition at medical centers throughout the metro area."

The report shifted to information about places to donate money to the memorials of the victims. In a moment of unbridled fear, Veronica wanted desperately to hold her son. *This can't be happening,* she thought.

A loud cry came from the other end of the room.

"That son-of-a-bitch should be hung! He's here! Let me find that murdering coward..." The man at the opposite end of the food court burst over to the TV and snatched the cord from its outlet. The television died instantly.

Veronica was startled and wanted to leave, but the man

just stood there, six feet from her table, facing the black screen. When he turned, she saw that his face was lined with streaks of tears. He was Michael and Michelle's father.

The silence was like a slow, eternal death. Then, a woman approached him. He turned, and they embraced each other, quietly sobbing. Marie mumbled under her breath, "Let's get out of here," and started to stand. Veronica stood, but not to leave. She approached the couple who were talking quietly by this time.

"Veronica, what are you doing?" Marie whispered, but didn't receive an answer.

"Mr. Harding," she said slowly. "I want you to know you have my deepest sympathy."

The man eyed her carefully as his wife glanced between them, confused.

"You may think you are alone with your fears and your sadness, but please believe me when I say, I know your pain unlike anyone else can. I truly do." She glanced at the woman. "And, please, don't hate Timothy. Don't think of him as a monster. We may never know why he did this, but we cannot hate each other."

"Who are you?" the woman asked.

Staring back, she replied, "The mother of a lost son." Veronica bowed her head and turned away slowly, walking toward the door.

"She's *his* mother! The killer's mother!" the woman gasped.

Before she could reach the door, Veronica felt an abrupt pull on her shoulder, which forced her to turn around.

Mr. Harding towered over her.

"Oh, I can hate," he said between clenched teeth. "I can

hate until the day I die. He took my son from us and tried to take our daughter. You have no right telling me what I can or cannot feel." He squeezed her arm tighter. "I don't care what you think you understand, because you don't. Your son is alive."

Marie gasped at how hard he was holding Veronica, but Veronica's eyes never faltered. His wife rushed over and pleaded with him to let go.

"You're wrong, Mr. Harding. My son died the moment he thought he could take a life," she said as she pulled her arm from his grasp.

Mrs. Harding stared at Veronica, seeing her own reflection as their eyes met. In that moment, she realized that whether or not this woman's son survived, they both had lost a child. She didn't want to feel sympathy for her, yet there it was. Ironically, the only other person who could truly understand what she and her husband were going through, was the mother of her son's killer.

Veronica and Marie quickly retreated to the private waiting room and sat in silence with their eyes closed. Their time for waiting was cut short when the door opened and the same doctor who explained her son's injuries that afternoon, entered with a solemn expression.

"Mrs. Thomas," he said in a heavy whisper. She nodded, and Marie reached for her hand.

"We tried our best to repair the damage, but it was just too much; his body couldn't take it." He paused to kneel beside the sobbing women.

"I'm so sorry, Mrs. Thomas."

In the days that followed the shooting, the news media surrounded the home of Veronica Thomas, pleading for a statement that she was unable to give so soon after the tragedy. Gradually, the attention died and when she spoke to the press, she expressed her indignation at how her son was depicted as a monster. He was not a monster. He was ill.

A few months after the shooting, the school erected a memorial statue with money raised throughout the state. It was a bronze statue of three children holding hands, each child representing a lost life.

Dedication

I'd like to dedicate this story to my three sisters, who have influenced my view of life. **Tyleen, the hopeful one**: you look to the future that I will have, standing by my side through some of the roughest times. You are always eager with a smile and a hug. **Charlene, the proud one**: you showed me, through your hard work and dedication, to strive for more than I have. **Ashley, the believer**: always so proud of my achievements. Your confidence in me helps me keep going, and you're never afraid to put me in my place.

Richard T. Camara

All Through the Night
by Richard T. Camara

Across the distant hills, the sun sets on another day. Many houses are filled with families sitting down to dinner, the world's troubles erased by their feelings of security. But one house feels no such joy. It sits upon a peaked hill with a deserted tire swing hanging from an oak tree, situated on the east side. The fall air has stripped the tree of its leaves, and from a window, a man watches it with sad eyes. Flashes of memories return.

A family sits upon a blanket underneath the tree; its shade is most welcome on this hot day. A laughing father is raiding the picnic basket. Even after all the previous scorns from his wife, he attempts to enter it once again. Laughter releases from the man as his daughter gives him a look of frustration. The ten-year-old looks to her mother for support. With a wink from her mother, they both tackle him, and in a tumble, the women reign supreme as they pin him to the lawn. Screams of unfairness ring from the man, seeping out through his laughter, but his cries are drowned under a flood of kisses.

Daylight fades again as the specters of the past disappear. Tears drift down his face, for once he was that man. The wheelchair he sits in faces the window and upon the sill sits a picture of his once family. Time was all he needed, friends and family had said. Time would dull the pain. Fools. The pain is as intense as the day he awoke in the hospital.

Cold metal massages his hand as he holds the pistol he bought to protect his family. For weeks he has planned this night, over and over. Since waking up in the hospital, he has thought mainly of ending it, even though people have tried to reach out to him. But, casually he ignores them all.

On that fateful night, he lost his family. Life was no longer worth living. The very things that gave him joy had been taken from him. Only God knew for what reason. But one memory of his wife kept him clinging to his existence.

A year ago, his Anna had found a lump in her breast. First, she had panicked, and it took all his calming to convince her to see the doctor. With his reassurance, managed to get through the tests and return home. They locked themselves in their room waiting for the call that would bring them the results, the call that would determine if she would die. In all his life, he had never been so frightened. Only at that moment, did he truly know fear.

She had turned to him and said the words that still rang in his head "If I die, you must promise me you will go on or at least try. Don't let the pain take you from this world." He told her not to say such things, that she would live, but the truth was, he feared her death too much to accept it.

"Please," she begged. "If I die, please just try, if not for me, for our daughter." Crying, she buried her head in his shoulder. All he could do was hold her and promise he would try, but never did she say anything about losing them both.

Anna cheated death that day. Benign is what the doctors called it, but death would have her and his daughter a year later.

The promise he made with himself was that he would "try" for his Anna. For the first time, he would replay that night's events. If it became too much, he would give up, but if he lived to see the sun rise again, he would give life a second chance. One last time he checked the bullet in the chamber and remembered.

The day had been warm; it was a Saturday, and they had gone to the beach. In the previous weeks, he had spent a lot of time at work, so he was repaying his family for their understanding. At dusk, they had packed their things into the car and headed home. Sounds of soft music played over the radio as he drove. His daughter slept in the back after a long day of fun and happiness. Every once in a while he would check on her by tilting the rear view mirror. Next to him, his wife spoke softly.

Passion was threaded through her every word. Her passion was what he first fell in love with. Everything she did was with determination. Sometimes she would get so worked up, he couldn't help but laugh. Shifting his vision to her, he interrupted her. Softly he said, "I love you." A smile brightened her face. Reaching up, she gently brushed her hand against his cheek. They drove on in silence, and he could feel her watching him.

Soon, she was fast asleep. The car turned onto a highway, and the shifting of the car leaned her toward him. Her head hung in the air with no support. The seatbelt restricted his movement, so he couldn't support her with his body. Reaching over, he unclasped his seatbelt and gently slid her head against him. That was the last happy memory he had.

His eyes catch the picture of his family, and his heart makes him "try" once again.

Driving at night had always bothered Anna. "All the lunatics come out after dark," she would say, and he would laugh. He wished he would have listened to her. Headlights flashed in his eyes as cars passed. The regular flow of lights from oncoming cars became one with the road. So familiar they became, that he thought nothing of the cars as they passed. Then, something caught his attention. Headlights were coming directly at them. Sitting up quickly, he realized too late, the fatal hand being dealt him.

Slamming on the brakes, he turned the wheel a hard right, trying to dodge the oncoming car. Instead of turning out of the car's way, their Ford Escort turned sideways, sliding into it. Screeching wheels sounded through the night, followed by a loud explosion.

Time moved in a blur. The oncoming car slammed head-on into the driver's side. In the air, his car flipped over and over. The world turned upside down. With wind whipping through his body, suddenly, he realized he had been thrown from the car. Colors flew and time spun as one moment turned into a timeless void. The impact came suddenly, and time began anew.

After a few moments, his eyes refocused. Lifting his head, a pain shot through his back. Ignoring it and the possibilities that came with it, he looked at his surroundings, searching for his family. Suddenly, light erupted, brightening the darkness. Fifty yards away, the source was evident; a fire burned around his car. The mangled shapes made no sense to his fogged mind, but reality hit quickly; the car was upside down. Through the illumination, he could see his family still within the car. Fear raced in his heart as he struggled to get up. The limbs that had faithfully served him, didn't respond; his legs were dead. Panic began to swell within him, as the fire grew closer to the car. Ignoring *the pain that followed, he used his arms to drag himself toward the inferno.*

The humming and crackling of the fire was broken by a desperate call. "DADDY!" Again and again it was called. Tears poured down his face as he urged faster. All the strength of his heart was forced into his arms, but it would not be enough.

Sweat beads upon his forehead as he screams into the night releasing the pent-up pain and anguish. With those emotions spent, he feels only an empty loss.

Metal flashes in an instant. The clicking of the hammer echoes in the empty room. Facing death is not at all what people said it would be, and a peaceful resilience shines through the darkness and unknown. Closing his eyes would be a mistake, he thinks; it might bring back their screams. He tries to remember their laughter and the love that once blessed him.

His finger becomes familiar with the trigger as it probes its edges. Then, a single beam of light strikes him, pausing his hand. Watching from the window, the horizon explodes with the sunrise and his life begins anew with the day. The gun drops to the floor.

* * * * * *

We all face tragedy in our lives. We have all felt helpless. It doesn't have to end in sadness. Hope, yes hope. There is always a dawning day, a twinkle of twilight. There is always a choice, a new day, and a new life.